Unity in Diversity

Melanie Lotfali

~ Credits ~

Author & Illustrator   Melanie Lotfali

Digital Editor   Michael Cohen

Books in this collection

God's Tais

NCREMENT OF

Atesa, Akala, Aleki, Zenha
and Abel love their parents.
One day they decide to make
a present for their parents.
They go to buy some cotton
to make tais.

Atesa's favorite color is green.
She makes a green tais.
Akala likes yellow.
She makes a yellow tais.

LET'S ENJOY WITH THE COLOR INCREMENT OF COLOR.
꽃이

Aleki's favorite color is red.
He uses red cotton to make
a tais for his parents.
Zenha thinks that pink is
the most beautiful.

Abel says that blue is the best.
He makes a blue tais.

When they finish their tais the
children go and play.
They leave the scraps of
cotton on the ground.
Ameta walks past and finds
the cotton left by the other
children. She uses the cotton
to make a tais.

Atesa's parents like the green tais that Atesa made for them.

Akala, Aleki, Zenha and Abel's parents also like the yellow, red, pink and blue tais that their children made for them.

But Ameta's parents were
the happiest of all because
their tais was made of many
different colors.

The people of the world are
many different colors.
Different colored cotton makes
a tais more beautiful.
And different colored people
make our world family more
beautiful.

The Earth is but
one country,
and mankind
its citizens.

~ Bahá'í Writings ~

The Eye that Wanted to Live Alone

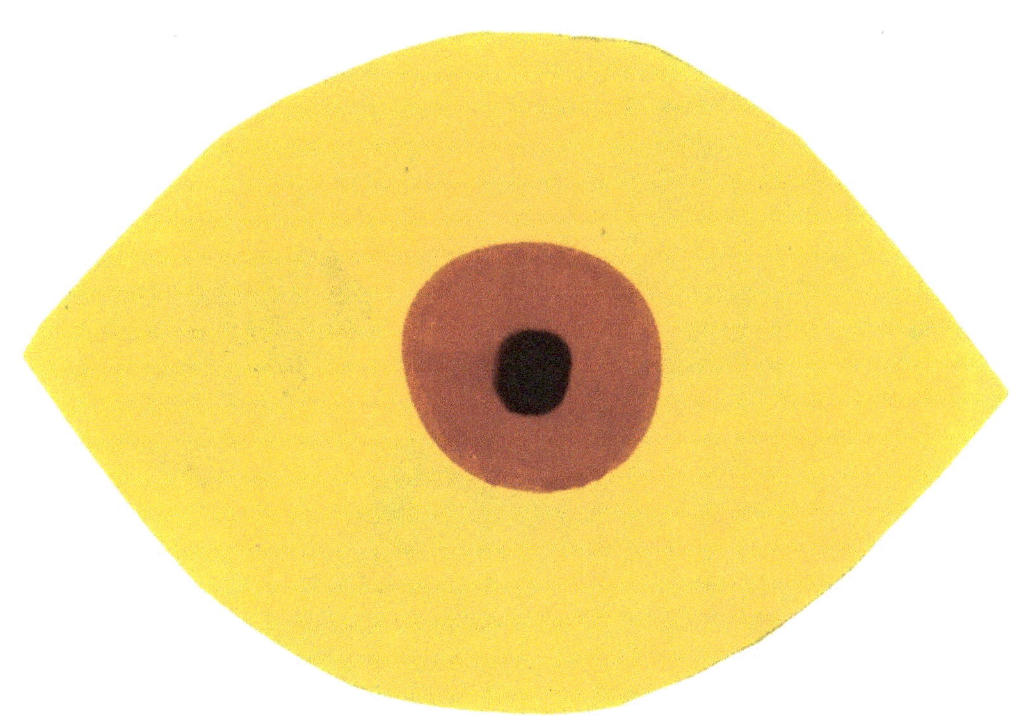

Once upon a time there lived a Body. This Body had all the things that bodies usually have, like two eyes, two hands, tummy, back, hair, ten fingers, and a bottom.

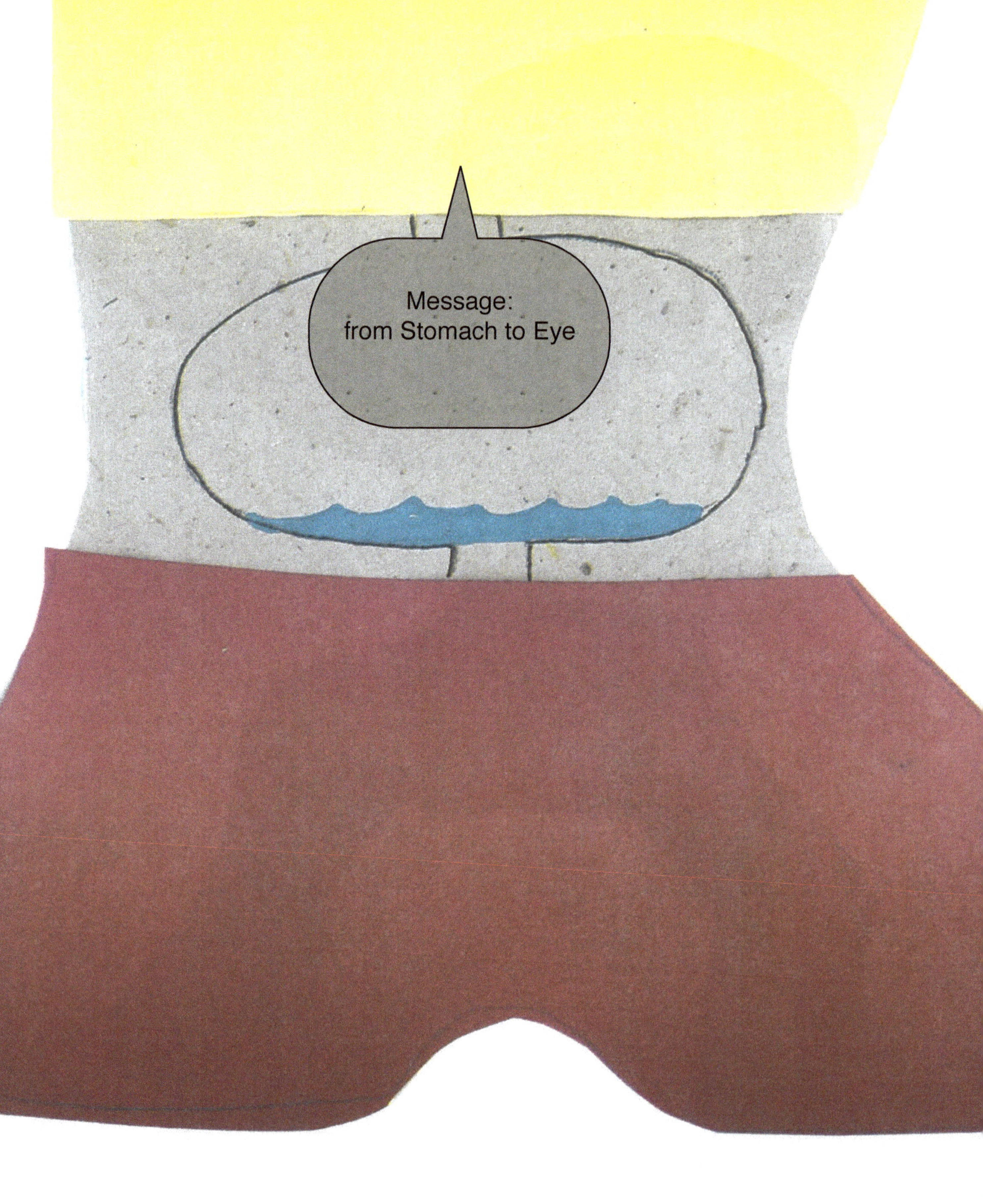

Message:
from Stomach to Eye

The parts of the Body were
different and played different roles
but they all worked together
successfully.

For example, when Tummy felt
empty, she told Eye to look for
something to eat.

Eye looked for food and then told Hand to take it. Hand took the food, Mouth opened and received the food. Teeth chewed the food and Tummy received the food. Tummy turned it into energy which it sent to Arms and Legs so that they could do their work. And so, all the parts of the body worked together in harmony.

But, one day, Eye started to think that she was more important than the other body parts. She thought: "If I don't look for food, Hand doesn't know where to get it. Then, Mouth doesn't know to open and Tummy stays empty. I am the most important!"

Eye ordered the other body parts to call her Queen Eye. She told them that she was the most important and they should honor her. But the other body parts didn't agree. They said to Eye: "No, we all need each other. We all help each other and depend on each other."

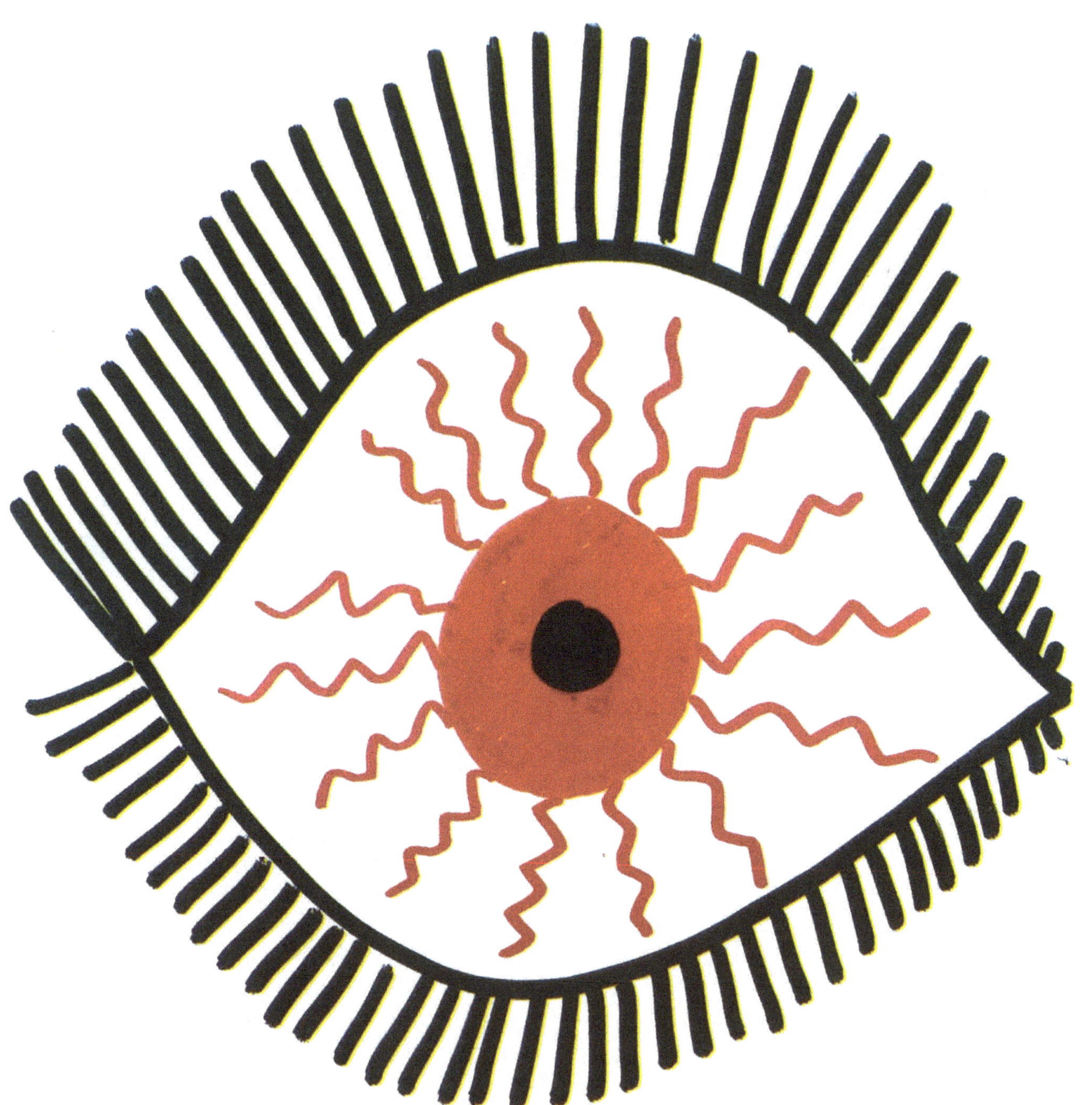

When Eye heard that they didn't accept that she was most important, she was angry!

She said: **"If you don't accept that I am queen, and if you don't honor me, I will not live with you!"**

Eye popped out of Face. She went

to live alone on the table top.

The body parts felt very sad that Eye didn't want to live with them. A couple of hours later, Tummy felt empty. She sent a message to Eye's place, but there was no Eye. So the message was sent directly to Hand. Hand received the message but didn't know what to do. He didn't know where to find food.

Hand began to look for food by feeling. This took a long time but in the end he found a banana and gave it to Mouth. Mouth received it. Teeth chewed it. Tummy turned it into energy and sent it to Arms and Legs. Body suffered, but it didn't die.

Meanwhile Eye sat alone on the table top. She sat and thought about how she was more important than the other parts. But after some time she also began to lose energy. Alone she could not get food, chew it or turn it into energy.

In the end she was about to die. She called the Body and said: "Help me please. I am about to die."

The Body said to Eye: "You are right. You can't live alone. We need your help and you also need us. Let's help each other." Hand picked up Eye and put her back in Face.

Eye began to receive energy from the food that Tummy received from Hand and Mouth. Eye didn't die. She felt happy.

Eye said sorry to the other parts and said: "I made a mistake. You were right. We should all work together. We are all important, and we need unity to live well together."

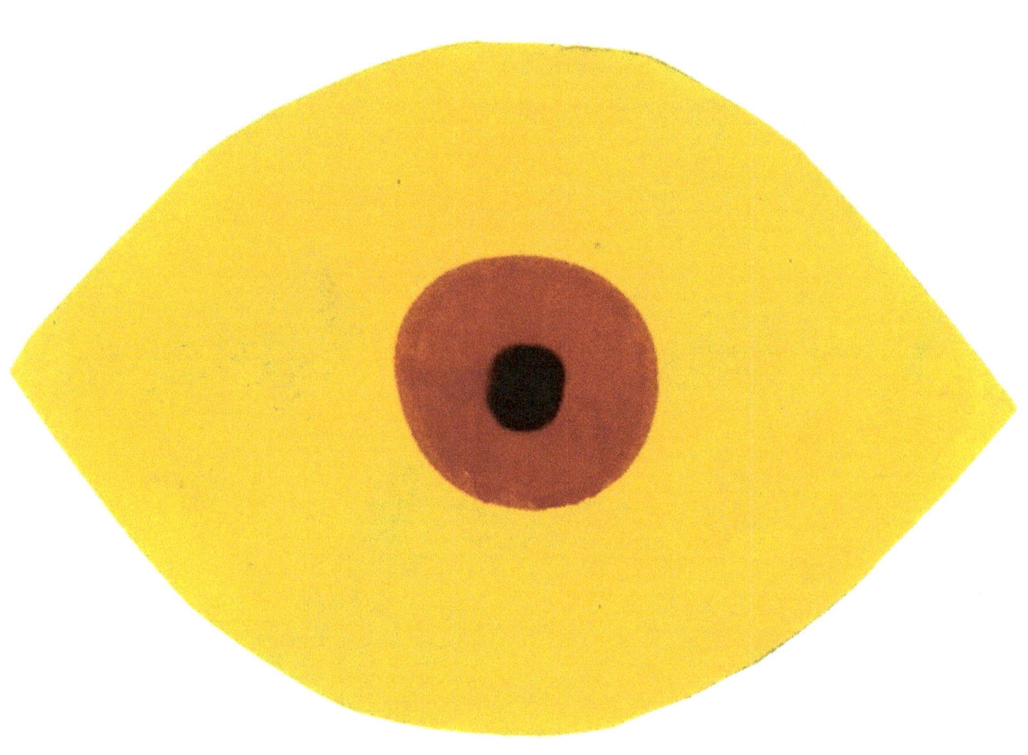

Be ye as the fingers
of one hand,
the members of
one body.

~ Bahá'í Writings ~

A Perfect Chord

Indi-bird loved to sing.
She knew how to sing one
note. She sang it beautifully
and with all her heart.

One day Jarrah-bird came
to visit. He also knew how
to sing one note.
They sang together.

Attracted by the sound,
Tai-bird landed on the
branch. He also knew how
to sing just one note. It was
different from the others.
He added his note
to the chord.

Marama-bird heard the
beautiful harmony of the three
different notes. "I can sing a
note too," she chirped.
She joined the group.

Tama-bird flew in with a long
loud "Cheeeeep Cheeeep".
Joyfully he added his note
to the music.

The harmony of the different notes was like a magnet for Mihi and Skye. They glided over to the branch. They opened their beaks and sang their notes. Each bird's note was different from the others. Each note was beautiful. Together they made the perfect chord.

The diversity in the human
family should be the cause
of love and harmony, as it
is in music where many
different notes blend
together in the making of
a perfect chord.

~ Bahá'í Writings ~

Stars of One Heaven

Clara was all alone. Clara was lonely.
She looked up at the sky. She saw
the sky was full of stars.

She turned to one and said: "You are
so lucky. You have so many friends.
I am all alone. I want a friend."

Star said: "Clara, why don't you ask
God for a friend?"

So Clara prayed. She asked God
to send her a friend.

When she opened her eyes she saw
that God had sent her a friend.

"Oh no!" said Clara. "I want a friend
just like me! He is different from me!"

Clara closed her eyes and prayed again. Then, she opened her eyes.

"Oh no!" sobbed Clara.

"I want a friend just like me! She is different from me!"

Clara closed her eyes and prayed
again. Then, she opened her eyes.

"Oh no!" cried Clara.
"I want a friend just LIKE ME!
She is DIFFERENT from me!"

Clara threw herself on the grass.
She cried and cried.
The new friends wandered away.

That night she turned to Star.
"Why does God keep sending me
the wrong thing?" she asked.

Star said to Clara: "When you look
up to the sky, what do you see?"

Clara said: "I see beautiful stars shining brightly."

Star said: "That's right. We are all different shapes, colors, and sizes. But when you look up you see our unity. You see we are all stars."

"When I look down," said Star,
"I see beautiful human beings.
It doesn't matter that you are
different shapes, colors, and sizes.
You are all human beings."

"Oh yes!" laughed Clara.
"Now, where did they go,
those friends just like me?"

....love will make
them all the stars
of one heaven.

~ Bahá'í Writings ~

The Fruit of One Tree

When I get up I see our fruit bowl. It is full of ripe yellow bananas. Today I want to eat bananas for breakfast, lunch, and dinner. I peel a banana and take a big bite.

Then I see Maria selling mangos. I remember how sweet and slimy they are. Maria sells me some mangos.

When I go to the tap to wash
the mango juice from my chin,
I see our paw paw tree.
Paw paw with lime juice.
My favourite!

Even with my belly full of paw paw, the orange tree catches my eye. I pull an orange off the branch. I peel it and break the orange ball into pieces. I put them in my mouth one by one.

I start to think: Bananas are yummy. Mangos are sweet. Paw paws are delicious. Oranges are tasty.

What if we put them together? What if we ate them mixed together? That would be the best of all.

Yummy, sweet, delicious,
tasty Fruit Salad!

O people of the
world, ye are all the
fruit of one tree
and the leaves of
one branch.

~ Bahá'í Writings ~

Fellowship Farm

Volume 1: BOOKS 1-3

Leezah, Skye-Maree and Olingah Fitzgerald live with their parents on Fellowship Farm. In the first book of the Fellowship Farm series, you will meet the children and learn about their daily activities on the farm. There is a lot to be done each day: pillow fights, morning prayers, pig feeding and school bus riding. They help their dad feed the cows, add stickers to their virtues poster and learn to deal with bullies.

Then you will join the Fitzgerald children on their many adventures with puppies, snake bites, treasure hunts, bonfires, camping by the sea, and tree houses. And as they go they sometimes practice their virtues, and sometimes forget…

Suitable for independent readers aged 8-12 years; parent-read from six years. Order online from print-on-demand services, and digitally from the iBookstore or Kindle.

Fellowship Farm

Volume 2: BOOKS 4-6

Leezah, Skye-Maree and Olingah Fitzgerald live with their parents on Fellowship Farm. In the first volume of the Fellowship Farm series, you met the children and learned about their daily activities on the farm.

In this the second volume the Fitzgerald children are visited by their cousins, Nick and Anisa. Together they travel by horse and cart to the market, attend the 19 Day Feast, go camping, find a pirate map and treasure, as well as experience the intensity of crisis and victory when Olingah's life is put in serious danger.

Suitable for independent readers aged 8-12 years; parent-read from six years. Order online from print-on-demand services, and digitally from the iBookstore or Kindle.

Fellowship Farm

Volume 3: BOOKS 7-9

In this, the third volume of stories about Leezah, Skye-Maree and Olingah Fitzgerald who live with their parents on Fellowship Farm, the children set out with joy to go blackberry picking.

But an unexpected turn of events at the river makes them fear for the lives of their puppies. Ayyám-i-Há follows with serving, teaching, gifts, treasure-hunts as well as the challenge of bullying for Skye-Maree. After Ayyám-i-Há comes an opportunity to visit their eccentric Uncle Jack who takes them to the chocolate factory, aquatic centre and gives them many other treats both spiritual and edible!

Suitable for independent readers aged 8-12 years; parent-read from six years. Order online from print-on-demand services, and digitally from the iBookstore or Kindle.

Fellowship Farm

Volume 4: BOOKS 10-12

In the fourth volume of stories about Leezah, Skye-Maree and Olingah Fitzgerald of Fellowship Farm they prepare for the annual Naw Ruz Mahta River Boat Race. There are some unexpected hitches.

Skye-Maree and Olingah learn about loyalty and sacrifice as they work out how to respond to the challenges they face. Soon after Naw Ruz winter sets in and the family rug up and head for the ski slopes.

Along the way they experience the life-threatening danger of losing unity, the challenge of learning to ski, the power of prayer, and patience in the face of frustration. They meet funny Magic, the back to front panda, and suffer some bruises. Their patience is well rewarded when their parents announce that a dear wish of the children is to be fulfilled.

Suitable for independent readers aged 8-12 years; parent-read from six years. Order online from print-on-demand services, and digitally from the iBookstore or Kindle.

Unity in Diversity

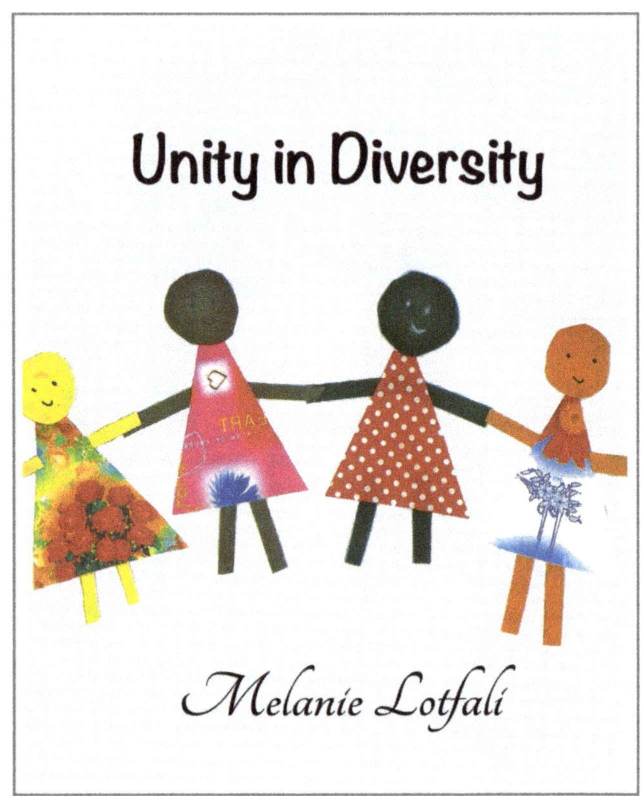

This brightly illustrated picture book contains five simple stories for young readers. They foster an understanding of the oneness of the human race and celebrate its diversity within that unity.

Likening the human race to various colored cotton in a woven cloth, various fruits on the tree of life, stars in the heavens, members of one body, and different notes in one perfect chord, the stories use the concrete to teach the abstract.

Young readers will enjoy the bright colors and simple text as they develop their understanding of the unity and diversity of the human race.

Ideal for children aged 4-8 years.
Order online from print-on-demand services, and digitally from the iBookstore. Translated into French, Portuguese, Romanian, Tetum, and Mongolian.

The Big Story

The Big Story explains the way in which the divinely ordained and guided process that has brought human beings into existence has taken place gradually over time and space. It shows that the concepts of evolution and creation are not mutually exclusive.

Science and religion are shown to be two windows on one reality, two knowledge systems that when properly understood, function as one cohesive whole.

This book is most suitable for readers 14 years and older. Younger readers will enjoy the bright and informative illustrations but will require support to understand the text.

Suitable for independent readers aged 14+ years; with assistance from 12+. Order online from print-on-demand services, and digitally from the iBookstore.

Dr Melanie Lotfali

Author of The Fitzgeralds of Fellowship Farm series and Unity in Diversity series.

Melanie Lotfali PhD is a graduate of the Australian College of Journalism in Professional Writing for Children. She is the author of eighteen books of fiction and non-fiction for children and the illustrator of five.

Melanie has taught spiritual education classes for children for the past twenty years in five countries and is currently an active animator and trainer of animators for the Junior Youth Spiritual Empowerment Program. She is a qualified counselor and classroom teacher, and for the past six years has facilitated violence prevention and respectful relationships programs in high schools.

Much of her childhood was spent on the farms, beaches and mountains of Tasmania, where the Fellowship Farm series is set. As an adult she spent four years in Siberia and four years in East Timor as a pioneer.

She currently lives in Lismore, Australia, with her family.

Michael Cohen

Author of The Big Story and publisher of all Michelangela books.

Michael Cohen graduated as a Computer Systems Engineer in 1990 and worked for many years in software design and informations systems. He changed careers in 2008 to become a Registered Nurse working in the area of Mental Health and Alcohol & Other Drugs.

Michael has been a keen participant in and advocate of the programs offered by **The Foundation for the Application and Teaching of the Sciences** (FUNDAEC) and **Institute for Studies in Global Prosperity** (ISGP). He strives to contribute to processes and discourses leading to the progress of humankind toward a world society characterized by unity, justice and equity. A fundamental premise of Michael's worldview is that true science and true religion are necessarily in harmony, indeed are two windows on one reality. His writing seeks to promote understanding of this liberating concept and to contribute to a civilization that is ever advancing materially and spiritually.

He currently lives in Lismore, Australia, with his family.

Michelangela

website - www.michelangela.com.au
email - info@michelangela.com.au

To receive Michelangela's occasional
product announcements
please visit our website and
enter your email address and name
via the subscribe button